HEMI:
a Mule

Harper & Row, Publishers

New York, Evanston, San Francisco, London

Weekly Reader Children's Book Club presents

HEMI:
a Mule
by Barbara Brenner

Pictures by J. Winslow Higginbottom

For Dick

Weekly Reader Children's Book Club Edition

Contents

To Begin With

When Mare and Jackass mated, anyone around the barnyard could have told you what was going to happen. And it did. Ten and a half months later, Mare gave birth to a fine baby mule.

Both parents were delighted. They decided to name the foal *Hemionus,* which is the Greek name for mule and means *half-ass.* They felt that giving him an ancient name would help him to grow up with a sense of his own history. "After all," Jackass observed proudly, "the breeding of mules is at least three thousand years old."

The other animals agreed that not only was Hemionus a good name for a mule, but that Hemi was as fine an example of his breed as had ever

been born around those parts. There was only one unpleasant note struck on that happy occasion. Hen was overheard to remark that it was her opinion that mules were obsolete. But since no one knew exactly what obsolete was, they paid no attention to her and the moment passed.

So there he was. Hemionus. Alive and kicking.

1 *Alive and Kicking*

The first time Hemi saw his reflection it came as something of a shock. It is hard enough to see yourself as you really are, but if you are young and looking into a scummy pond, it is at least twice as hard.

"Can that be me?" he asked his father, who was grazing nearby.

"No one else but," Jackass replied.

"Well," said Hemi, peering through the algae, "all I can say is—either my ears are too long and my legs are too short, or my tail is too short and my body is too long."

"That's a matter," his father observed, "of your being neither horse nor jackass."

"How come?" Hemi wanted to know.

"I'm glad you asked that question," said his father, settling down for a long talk.

"You see," he began, "if your mother is a horse and your father is a horse, then . . . you're a horse. Howsoever, if both your father and your mother are jackasses, that is, donkeys, you're always bound to be a jackass. Like me. But," he concluded, coming to the point, "anyone whose mother is a mare horse and whose father is a jackass, is always—and forever—and definitely—a mule. Now that's a fact of life."

"That's interesting," said Hemi. "Tell me more."

"Well, now," said Jackass, pleased that his son had such a curious mind, "perhaps I should tell you about the hinny, whose father is a horse and whose mother is a jackass . . . or the case where . . ."

He was interrupted by Mare, who had been standing nearby listening. "I think that's quite enough facts of life for one day," she said firmly. "You're telling him more than he needs to know.

"Come home and eat now," she said sweetly to Hemionus. "We'll talk later."

So Hemi trotted into the barn after his mother and she nursed him. As he drank, she nuzzled his ear and said softly, "The important thing to remember is that you are what you are. So make the most of it."

The little mule burped sleepily, full of mother's milk and new ideas.

4

༄༅༅༄

The farm where Hemi spent his early years was a good place. It had green fields and a river view and plenty of mounds of rough earth for a mule to roll on and scratch his back. It also had a cozy barn where he could go when it rained and find dry oats and good company.

Hemionus loved the barn. He liked the snugness of the stalls in the back, and the way the sun streamed through the open door in the front. He liked the smell of rotting hay and musty corners, and the sound of animals stamping and swishing, and the twitter of barn swallows over his head. In fact, there was nothing that Hemionus didn't like about the barn. Unless maybe it was Hen, and even she was unpleasant only when she was hatching a brood.

The pasture was just as nice as the barn, but in a different way. If he wanted to, Hemi could stand by the pasture fence and watch the pickup trucks going into town and coming back along the high-way. Or he could chase a butterfly or two down in the meadow. Or pick himself out a nice young sassafras tree and strip the tender leaves from it. There was no end to the things a young mule could find to do in the pasture.

In the spring, when the dandelions were in bloom, the pasture was a carpet of yellow. Later, in clover time, it was a sea of lavender and white, and the soft

drone of bees filled the air. In the summer, the pasture was blue with chicory, and white with Queen Anne's lace.

"You never get tired of one color before another one comes in," Hemi observed one morning as he stood in the pasture chewing a stalk of chicory.

"True enough," his mother said, "and the best part is, it's all edible. Try the crown vetch," she urged him. "Have some alfalfa. Sample the soybean—it's full of protein."

So Hemi ate. And enjoyed. And grew. And then ate some more. And so on. By the time he was six months old, he was eight hands high, hard of hide, sound of tooth, and a tribute to his mother's fine care.

But while Hemi was building his body, he didn't neglect to feed his mind. He tagged along after his father, asking him all sorts of questions.

He started by asking *what?* In this way he learned the names of things—like the parts of his body— *haunch* and *croup* and *withers.* He even learned *fetlock joint,* which is part of a mule's leg and happened to be where Hemi had a white star-shaped mark.

Next Hemi began to ask *where?* And his father taught him *over the hill* and *under the sycamore tree* and even *behind your left ear.*

But after a while Hemi began to ask *why?* "Why is a bird?" he asked. And, "Why do stars?" Now

8

why is the hardest question to answer. It was certainly too much for Jackass.

"*Why*," Hemi's father said firmly, "is almost always troublesome. You have to find the answers to *why* on your own."

"Why?" asked Hemi.

Jackass changed the subject.

That night his father and mother had a talk about Hemi.

"I think we have produced a very unusual offspring," said Jackass.

"You're right. He's deep," said Mare.

"Do you suppose all mules are this way?"

"I don't know," said Mare.

"I think that youngster will go places," his father decided.

It wasn't long after this that Jackass left the farm. It happened suddenly; he hardly had time to say good-bye to his son. But he managed to give Hemi some last-minute advice.

"Beware of small yapping dogs and large wild boys," he said to Hemi just before they led him away. "The one will nip at your heels and the other will try to ride you."

"Above all," he added as he walked toward the U-Haul truck, "don't be put upon!"

"What does *put upon* mean, Papa?" Hemi called back.

"It means don't let them put too much upon you. Stand up for your rights. Be stubborn."

Hemionus was not at all sure what his father meant, but it was too late to find out. The doors of the truck swung closed and in a few minutes the truck was a speck faraway down the dusty road.

"Where did Papa go?" Hemi asked Mare that evening.

"He left for Parts Unknown," she answered.

"Where are Parts Unknown?" Hemi wanted to know.

"If I knew that, they wouldn't be Parts Unknown," his mother answered.

Hemi had a feeling he wasn't going to see his father again. *Why?* he wondered. Then he remembered. *Why* is almost always troublesome.

2 Melville

By the time Hemi was three years old, his father was no more than a pleasant memory. His mother had mated with Stallion and produced a new foal who took up most of her time. So Hemi hung around the barn and the pasture, keeping his eyes open and his ears likewise.

That fall he got his second teeth and did a lot more growing. By the following spring, he was fourteen hands high, he weighed nine hundred pounds, and he was getting restless. Growing, Hemi began to think, should not take up all of a mule's time.

"I'm sick of hanging around," he confided one day to Cow. "Everyone has something to do but me. . . ."

"Shucks, I don't do all that much," Cow said modestly. "Giving a little milk twice a day is no big accomplishment."

"I happen to think it's terrific," said Hemi admiringly. "Milk is a very important food, you know. Almost pure protein, Mama said. *I* think anyone who can give milk is quite special."

"Ahem!" said Hen, from the rafters. "Don't forget about me when you're passing out the praise. Those eggs I lay have a few proteins in them, too, you know."

"Oh, I know it. I was just about to say that," said Hemi, anxious not to offend the short-tempered Hen. "The laying of an egg is a remarkable achievement. That's just it. You lay eggs, Cow gives milk, my mother produces foals that Mr. Parkhurst can sell—I'm the only one who doesn't have anything to do."

"Patience, Hemi," said his mother. "You'll soon be old enough to do something useful."

"Amen to that," Hen clucked.

The next day, Melville arrived.

Melville was tall and skinny. He wore blue-jean overalls and a faded red shirt with the sleeves cut out. You could see muscles on Melville's arms. And his skin was smooth and brown. But it wasn't so much the way Melville *looked* as the way Melville *was*. There was something about Melville—the way he moved—and the way he looked at them—as if he were really seeing every one of them. Whatever

12

it was, the minute Melville walked into the barn that April morning, all the animals sat up and took notice.

"Hey, now," Melville announced, in a deep, rich voice, "my name's Melville. Come to help with the chores. Feed you up and clean you out." He got busy right away. As he talked, he swept and dumped, swung the clean hay down from the loft, and put out the feed for Hen. Then he got out the stool and began to milk Cow, but not before he'd gentled her with his hands and talked to her softly. When she was all quieted down and the milk was flowing, Melville did something unusual. He said softly, "How about we tune up a little?" Then Melville began to sing. In a moment, the barn was filled with beautiful sounds.

The animals had never heard music before. But they knew that the lovely sounds were coming straight from the inside of Melville. What a marvelous boy, thought Hemi, to be able to make sounds like that come from inside of him.

After Melville began to sing, you could have heard a piece of straw drop on the barn floor. Stallion stopped stamping his hooves on the floor. Hen stopped pecking and clucking. Cow didn't even swish her tail, she was so spellbound by the music of Melville. All you could hear was the sound of the milk going into the pail and the wonderful sound coming out of Melville.

When Melville departed, he left behind him a

clean barn and the most pleasant vibrations.

All the animals began to talk at once.

"Now that is what I call a pleasant young man," said Cow. "Such gentle hands."

"I've never seen the barn so neat," said Mare, who was fussy about keeping her children in a clean place.

"Fine boy," said Stallion heartily, and Rooster crowed his agreement.

From then on, Melville came to the barn every day. The more Hemi saw of him, the more he liked him. Besides the fact that Melville kept the barn shipshape, and never let the feed get moldy, he had other special qualities. He had a fine hand for scratching a mule in the right places. And he always carried a bit of something sweet in his pocket for Hemi to munch on. But it wasn't even that Melville gave Hemi goodies. It was far deeper than that. Hemi and Melville had a special feeling for each other. They were friends.

Soon, Melville got in the habit of wandering down to the barn at night. He'd come to Hemi's stall and after he'd given Hemi a Milky Way, or an Oh Henry, he'd sit down in Hemi's stall and talk to him. Hemi loved those evenings. Sometimes Melville would say, "Hey, man, let's tune up a little." And he'd sing. Softly, so that it wouldn't disturb the other animals. And the two of them would sit there, enjoying. Sometimes he'd even tell Hemi about a song. "Hey, man," he'd say. "Listen to this one. This one's

Rhythm and Blues." Or, "This is Folk Rock, man." Or, "Wanna hear a little Country and Western?" Melville knew every kind of song. Sometimes he'd sing the words to a song while he was stroking Hemi's neck or his withers in time to the music.

At other times, he'd just sit there quietly. After a while Hemi would put his head in Melville's lap. Then Melville would talk to him and tell him about his plans.

"Man, I'm going to go away from here someday," he'd say. "I'm going to get myself an education. Take myself down to that Agricultural College in Tucson, Arizona. Learn how to be a real farmer, is what I'm gonna do.

"And when I do," he'd say, coming to the part that Hemi liked best, "when I do, I'm going to get me a place. Then I'm gonna buy you from Mr. Parkhurst, and you and me are gonna have our own farm. Together."

Hemi would nibble Melville's knee gently to show him that he was paying attention.

One spring morning Melville came into the barn earlier than usual. As soon as he had finished milking the cow and cleaning out the stalls, he came over to Hemi. In his hand he had a loop of leather with a piece of metal attached to it. He held it out for Hemi to see and sniff.

"Hey, looka here. This here's your bit and halter. Ain't nobody but you belongs to that, man. That's yours. You gonna put that on you now, jest like a grown-up mule, and your Mama's sure gonna be proud of you."

Slowly, he slid the leather up on Hemi's neck, all the while talking to him soothingly. When he slipped the leather piece over Hemi's head, the mule was surprised, but he didn't object. He knew Melville wouldn't do anything that was bad for him. But when Melville put the cold metal bit in his mouth, Hemi balked. He jerked his head down sharply, and discovered that that thing hurt when you pulled against it. He looked at Melville reproachfully.

"Well, now, man, if you're gonna pull your head, you ain't gonna be comfortable. Jest you hold still and take it easy." Melville's voice soothed Hemi and he stood quietly.

"Okay, now, let's move on out," said Melville quietly, and he began to lead Hemi out of the stall by the halter. As he did, he sang softly:

> *"Had a mule and her name was Sal,*
> *Fifteen miles on the Erie Canal."*

Calmed by Melville's velvet voice, Hemi followed him. They walked round and round the corral, Melville singing and the mule following in his footsteps.

Hemionus had been broken to the bit and halter.

But that was only the first step in his training. After they had walked around like that for a few mornings, Melville put a saddle on Hemi and got on his back. Hemi was so startled that he sat right down.

"Hey, man, don't lay down on the job. Get up. We got places to go. Come on, baby." Melville coaxed and cajoled and bribed. Two hours and four Milky Ways later, Hemi had been broken to the saddle.

It remained only for him to learn to pull the plow. Thanks to Melville's kindness and patience, it wasn't long before he learned that, too. Once he got the hang of it, Hemi really *liked* pulling the heavy plow. Everyone around the farm remarked about his strength for his age, and about the fact that he had such pride in his work.

Melville never stopped telling him, "Man, you are one smart mule. No one but a smart mule like you coulda learned to do that so fast." The more Melville told him what a terrific worker he was, the more Hemi was a terrific worker.

That spring, Hemi and Melville plowed out a whole new field over on the north side of the farm. Together they turned it and furrowed it and sowed yams and beans and cabbage and turnips and tomatoes.

Hemi learned to love plowing. He learned to love the smell of the rich earth and the feeling of it under his hooves. He liked the way it looked when the plow turned it over—black, and alive with earthworms and other tiny creatures of every description.

All through the spring Melville and Hemi sowed the crops, to the tune of "Had a mule and her name was Sal . . ."

All through the long, hot summer they cultivated, to the tune of "Shenandoah," and "Swing Low, Sweet Chariot," and "Mockingbird."

All through the late summer and fall, they picked the vegetables and took them to market, to the tune of "Haul Away, Joe," and "The Erie Canal."

Then, before they knew it, it was going on winter, and although there were plenty of songs left to sing, there were no more crops to pick.

Both Hemi and Melville were sad to have it end.

"Well, now, you just take yourself a rest, man," Melville advised. "You just have yourself a little vacation."

So Hemi rested in the warm barn, proud of his season's work. And Melville went to town to finish high school. Every Saturday Melville came to work at the farm. All the animals looked forward to Saturday, but none of them as much as Hemi.

One day toward the end of winter, Melville appeared at the barn door dressed in a shirt and tie and permanent-press pants. As soon as Hemi saw him, he knew that it was some kind of special day.

"Man," Melville said, all excited, "you won't believe what has happened to me. I got me a scholarship. To the Agricultural College at Tucson, Arizona. Going to get that education."

Hemi tried to act pleased because he knew it was what Melville wanted. But all he could think of was that Melville was going away. Melville saw how Hemi felt, and after passing him two Oh Henry bars for comfort, he said, "Well, now. I'll be back. I mean it, man. I'll be coming back on vacation to visit you. And one day, when I finish school, I'm coming back to get you. You better believe it."

Hemi believed it because he wanted with all his heart to believe it. But still he had a few difficult moments when Melville drove away in the old pickup truck.

"There certainly is a lot of coming and going in my life," Hemi said sadly. "Mostly going."

3 *Gravely Tractor*

Hen was in a cranky mood. She was brooding again, and that always affected her disposition, which was none too good to begin with.

Hemi, on the other hand, was feeling quite cheerful. Spring was coming again and he was looking forward to getting back to work. He remembered with pleasure the smell of newly turned earth, and the look of a straight furrow and a sprouting seed. He thought of walking along with his strong back pulling the plow, while someone walked behind him, sowing seeds and singing about the mule named Sal.

"I wonder what the new boy will sing," he said to Cow.

"Sing when?" asked Cow.

"While we're plowing. Melville used to sing folk songs. I think Folk music is just right for plowing, don't you? I do like Classical and even a little Rhythm and Blues now and then. But not for plowing. Folk songs are for plowing, don't you think so?"

"I guess so, Hemi. You know more about music than the rest of us," said Cow, in her generous way.

Suddenly Hen said, "What makes you think you'll be plowing this year?"

"Melville said plowing and planting and harvesting has to be done every year," said Hemi innocently.

"Don't be too sure, Sonny," said Hen.

"What do you mean by that?" asked Hemi.

"What I mean is what I say. Gravely," said Hen.

"You are saying it *gravely*, but I wish you could make it a little *clearer*," said Hemi.

"Don't pay any attention to her, Hemi," said Mare. "I'm certainly glad that I don't get like her when I'm about to become a mother."

The very next day, as Hemionus stood with Cow on the pasture slope, feeling the first warm rays of the spring sunshine, they heard the loud whirr of a motor. They looked over toward where the sound was coming from and saw a huge red machine moving back and forth in the north field like some giant red insect. The new boy was riding it.

Hemi and Cow hurried over to the fence to watch. It zoomed by, churning up the dirt as it passed. As it went by, Hemi distinctly saw the lettering on its

22

side: GRAVELY. When it went back the other way, he saw on its other side, TRACTOR.

"So that's it," said Hemi. "That's what Hen was talking about. A Gravely Tractor. I've been replaced by a machine."

"Now, now," said Cow soothingly. "Don't jump to conclusions. Maybe the tractor is just going to do the plowing. Maybe you'll get to do the seeding and the cultivating."

But in the days that followed, it became more and more clear that the machine was doing everything that Hemi had once done.

"It's just not fair," said Hemi despairingly to his friends in the barn. "Barely four years old and I'm already a has-been."

"It's because you're *obsolete*," said Hen from her perch. "I told your mother that a long time ago."

"What does obsolete mean?" Hemi asked.

"It means there's nothing a mule can do that a machine can't do better and faster.

"You see," Hen went on, in her patronizing way, "some things can't be replaced by a machine. For instance, no machine can lay an egg. But you, Sonny . . ."

"What will they do with me if I'm obsolete?"

"They'll send you off to the Meat Packer," Hen said matter-of-factly. "Dog food and fertilizer, you know."

Mare cut in quickly. "Pay her no mind, Hemi," she said. "She's being purely mean. I do wish she'd have those chicks and get it over with. She's impossible when she's been cooped up on a clutch of eggs for a while."

Hemi wasn't satisfied. He pressed his mother for more information. But she just shook her head and looked worried.

He went to Cow.

"Tell me what Hen meant," he begged.

Finally, Cow told him. "I don't know all the details," she said hesitantly, "but I have heard . . . uh . . . that some mules . . . uh . . . some, not all, you understand, are . . . uh . . . killed and

24

ground up for . . . uh . . . dog food and fertilizer. I believe," she said in her quiet way, "that that . . . uh . . . might have been what Hen was referring to."

"Mother Nature!" cried Hemi. "*Dog* food! *Fertilizer!* That's horrible!"

"Tut, tut, Sonny," said Hen, "it's the way of the world. I'll be someone's chicken dinner when my laying days are over."

"But . . . but . . . I'm *young*," Hemi blurted out. "I don't deserve to die."

Hen flew into a rage.

"I suppose I'm old," she snapped. "I suppose *I* deserve to end my days swimming in gravy. Covered with dumplings. I suppose it's all right for me to be boiled and minced with mayonnaise and celery. But you—I suppose—you're special. Oh, the young are cruel," she sighed, ruffling her feathers.

"I didn't mean . . . you shouldn't be manced with myonnaise . . . I mean minced with mayo . . . I mean, no one should be killed. Certainly no one I know," Hemi added desperately. "And there's no one I know better than me," he added, with a sob in his voice.

"There, now," said Cow. "No reason to look on the worst side of things. What I venture to say will happen is that Mr. Parkhurst will sell you to someone who doesn't have a Gravely Tractor."

"Do you really think so?" Hemi asked, hanging on Cow's words.

"Indeed I do," mooed Cow.

"I say only time will tell," said Hen.

Time told sooner than anyone expected. Hemionus woke the next morning to see Mr. Parkhurst and a strange man standing in front of his stall. They were talking about him.

"He *is* a fine mule. Nice straight back. Healthy looking."

Hemi looked at the stranger's olive-green uniform.

Who is he? Hemi wondered. He thought immediately of what Hen had said. Can it be the Meat Packer? So soon?

The man ran his hand expertly along Hemi's flanks. Hemi jumped.

"He's solid meat," said the man approvingly. "Not an ounce of fat on him."

Hemi almost fainted. Solid meat. No fat. It *was* the Meat Packer!

He shivered, and twisted his head to look reproachfully at Mr. Parkhurst, who seemed to avoid his eye.

"He seems a bit high-strung and nervous," the Stranger said.

Wouldn't you be nervous if you were being measured for the meat grinder? thought Hemi bitterly.

He heard Mr. Parkhurst assure the Stranger that Hemionus was gentle, even-tempered, *and* intelligent.

Do you have to be all that to be eaten? Hemi wondered. Do bad-tempered mules give a dog a bellyache? He had a sudden repulsive vision of some nasty little Pekingese eating him, and then getting cramps. He shuddered.

Now the uniformed stranger was looking into his mouth.

"I think they're going to grind up every part," Hemi muttered sadly. "Teeth. Tongue. Nothing will be wasted." He had a mighty impulse to bite the Meat Packer on the nose, but by the time he had examined all the pros and cons, the nose had moved out of reach.

"Well, I think he'll make a fine addition," the man said to Mr. Parkhurst. "If you don't mind, I'll take him right away."

"But I *do* mind," cried Hemi. "I want to say good-bye to my friends. I want to get in touch with Melville. I want . . ."

He brayed in anguish, but they seemed not to notice.

Mr. Parkhurst and the Stranger talked for a few minutes, and Hemi and the other animals strained to hear what they were saying. At one point, Mr. Parkhurst said something, and the Stranger laughed and said, "Don't worry. We'll slaughter them this year."

Hemi felt faint.

When the Stranger drove away in the jeep, Hemi noticed that the man who was driving him had a helmet which had M.P. on it. Meat Packer, thought Hemi in despair.

He threw himself down on the floor of the barn, his head against the dear, rough, familiar wooden floor. This was the first floor he had walked on after he was born. It was the very same floor that Melville had sat on during those long winter nights of singing and talking. And now that was all over. He would never see Melville again. Never, never. . . .

He sobbed, "This is it. No way out. Finished. Over. The end."

The other animals looked on sympathetically.

"I can't believe it," said Cow. "Mr. Parkhurst has always seemed like such a nice man."

Mare began to sniffle.

Then came a voice from the rafters. It was Hen. "Now stop all the carrying on," she said. "It isn't at all the way you think."

"Then what way is it?" asked Hemi morosely.

"Look, Sonny," said Hen. "See that jeep over there? That is a U.S. Army truck. You are being bought by the U.S. Army."

"You mean they're going to feed me to the *soldiers*?"

"No, Sonny. You're going to be their *mascot*. The Army football team has a mule for a mascot."

"I don't know what a football team is," Hemi said, with dignity. "And I don't know what a mascot is, either. But I do know this. I *heard* that Meat Packer say that they were going to slaughter me this year."

Hen clucked. "He meant slaughter Navy. That's another football team."

28

"You mean football teams eat each other?"

"No, no. My, you are ignorant. They play against each other and try to win. Slaughter is just an expression."

Hemi was weak with relief. "So you mean I am not to be killed?"

"Not on your life," said Hen.

4 Jackson

"It's just as hard to say good-bye when *you're* going as it is when someone else is going," Hemi decided the next morning.

All the animals were crowded around him, offering last-minute encouragement and advice. Stallion was urging him to take advantage of his opportunities. Cow was telling him how much she was going to miss him. Even Hen was all sweetness. "I hope you'll be very happy at the Academy, Sonny," she said. "You always were a nice boy."

"The important thing," he said to his mother for the tenth time, as she walked him to the door, "is that Melville should know where to find me."

His mother promised for the tenth time that Melville would know.

And she had her own advice for her son.

"Now, Hemi, make sure that you eat well. I've heard that Army food is terrible. You just kick up a fuss if they don't feed you right. And don't stand in drafts, remember that."

The truck was waiting. A moment later, Hemi was in the van. As the motor started, he thought, They've just got to remember about Melville.

They took Hemi for a long ride in the truck. Then he was put aboard a train and taken for an even longer ride.

After that, he was put in a truck again and taken for a short ride. At last, he arrived at his new home.

When the truck pulled up to the barn, someone was waiting for him. A man in a white coat, who he later found out was Dr. Timothy, the post veterinarian.

"Welcome home," the doctor said to the man in the green uniform, who led Hemi from the truck. "So this is our new one, eh?" The doctor patted Hemi in a friendly way. "Nice-looking fellow. What's his name?"

"Has a funny foreign name, sir," said Green Uniform. "Something with an H. I've forgotten."

"Well, it doesn't matter," said the veterinarian. "We always change their names, anyway. Let's pick a name for him right now."

"How about John James, for General Pershing, sir?" said Green Uniform.

"Nope. Too common."

"We could call him Ulysses, for General Grant, sir."

"Too uncommon."

"I have it," said the doctor. "Why don't we name him for that Revolutionary War General, Richard Henry Lee. The one they called Lighthorse Harry Lee. By golly, that's it. We'll call him Lighthorse Harry. After General Lee."

He chuckled and went into his office to make out an original paper and seventeen copies on the new mule.

Meanwhile, Hemi was muttering, "Lighthorse Harry? Light*horse* Harry? Is that a name for a mule?"

They led Hemi to a large corral in front of a big square barn. When they opened the gate, Hemi, knowing what was expected of him, walked in, and they closed the gate behind him.

"There you go, Harry," said Green Uniform, in a not unfriendly way, as he closed the gate.

So, thought Hemi. This is my new home.

For a moment he stood still, sniffing the air and looking around him. All around him, below this hill on which the barn and pasture stood, were the brick and sandstone buildings of the Academy. He could look down the hill and see the roads winding through the big military college. Below them, he could just make out the four-lane highway and the cars crawling like little bugs. And way off in the distance, he could see the river.

Hemi took a deep breath. He smelled clover, merion bluegrass, and an assortment of unidentifiable fescues. So far, so good in the smell department, he thought.

He took a few experimental nibbles at the pasture grass. It was sweet and crisp. "I think I'll like it here, pasturewise," he decided.

Now he saw something moving near the fence at the other end of the corral. He moved toward it, curious. When he got a little closer, the unmistakable smell of a fellow animal was borne to his nostrils. And then, as its outline became clearer . . .

"Can it be?" His ears twitched. "It is! Someone just like me! A fellow-mule!"

Overjoyed, Hemi scampered toward the stranger, planning what he would say.

"Let's see. I'll say, 'Hi, fellow-mule. You're a sight for sore eyes.' "

But when he thought about that, he decided maybe that wasn't the thing to say. Maybe the mule wouldn't know that expression and would think he, Hemi, had sore eyes.

Maybe a hearty approach would be better, he thought. How about if I say, "Hi, fellow-mule, whaddya say?" He tried it aloud. But that didn't seem quite right, either. Hemi was so nervous and anxious to find just the right words of greeting that

33

before he knew it he was across the pasture and standing directly in back of the strange mule. He decided quickly to just do the "Hi, fellow-mule" part of his speech and let the rest of the conversation develop naturally. But he had barely gotten out "Hi, fellow . . ." when he found himself flying through the air and landing in a not-too-soft bunch of thistles.

Words left his head entirely.

Hemi lay in the tall grass, dazed. In a certain way, he admired the speed with which the other mule's back legs had moved. In a certain other way, he was insulted, annoyed, and in pain.

"Why?" he demanded in an injured tone. "Just why?"

The big mule turned slowly.

"A mule does not like to be snuck up on," he said slowly.

"Well, I certainly didn't mean to give you that idea. I was just coming over to say 'Hi, fellow-mule' and things of that sort."

"Yes. Well. I'm sorry. I trust there are no bones broken."

The big gray mule helped Hemi to a standing position.

"You are my first fellow-mule that I have ever met in my whole life," said Hemi. "And so far, meeting a fellow-mule has not been pleasant."

"Believe me, I *am* sorry," the older mule said again. "I didn't mean for us to get off to such a bad

34

start. Please don't take it personally." And then, as if anxious to change the subject, he said, "You must be the new mule. I'm happy to meet you. My name is Jackson, what's yours?"

"Hemionus," said Hemi. "You may call me Hemi for short."

"But not for long," said Jackson.

"What do you mean?"

"I mean it's not likely that they'll let you keep your name. They mostly name us after generals or commanders-in-chief or some such warrior types. Jackson, for example, is for Stonewall Jackson. Civil War, you know."

"As a matter of fact, they did say something about calling me Harry, after a certain General Lee. However, they may call me what they like, but my *name* is Hemionus," Hemi said firmly.

"Then that's what I shall call you," said Jackson, anxious to make up to Hemi. "I shall always call you Hemionus. Hemi for short.

"Now, then," he said briskly. "That's settled. Next question is, what can I do for you? I'm prepared to make you feel at home in whatever way I can."

Hemi thought a minute.

"I'd like to learn something about this place. But," he added, "since you are a fellow-mule, what I'd really like is to learn everything I can about mules."

"Excellent," said Jackson. "Everything about something and something about everything. We'll start tomorrow, right after breakfast. How does that suit?"

"Perfect," said Hemi. "And speaking of mealtimes, the first thing I'd like to know is—when do we eat? I'm starved."

"Come this way," said Jackson. He led the way to the barn, where Hemi was put into a roomy stall, and both mules were given a fine dinner of mashed oats mixed with a little molasses.

"Mmmmm. Delicious. This is certainly a well-run place," said Hemi, with his mouth full. He looked around at the big, clean barn. "Tell me," he asked, "do we have the barn all to ourselves?"

"Yes, usually. Unless one of the officers wants to board his dog, or one of the cavalry horses gets sick. Most of the time we're alone. And very cozy it is, too. Plenty to eat, vacation all spring and summer, and . . ."

"Vacation spring and summer? But I don't understand. Spring and summer is planting time. How can we have time off during planting season?"

Jackson shook his head, chuckling.

"I can see that you have a lot to learn, my young friend. And the first thing I'll have to teach you is what it means to be a mascot to the Army football team."

"Oh, yes, do tell me," said Hemi. "Is it like plowing? I'm good at plowing. In fact, it's the only thing I know how to do so far," he added.

"It's *nothing* like plowing," said Jackson. "Now go to sleep. Lessons begin tomorrow."

Hemi closed his eyes, but he was thinking too much to sleep. Mostly he was thinking about Melville.

A few minutes later, he called softly to the next stall.

"Jackson."

No answer.

"Jackson. Do you like music? Do you like Dixieland? Folk Rock?"

Still no answer.

"Jackson? If a certain person came to the Academy looking for a certain mule, would he be able to find me?"

There was only the sound of snoring.

Oh, well, thought Hemi. I'll ask him the first thing tomorrow.

5 Lessons

The following day, Jackson told Hemi a lot about the Academy. Hemi learned that the Academy was a school where most of the people were called cadets. They had straight backs and short hair, they liked football, they were studying war, and the barns where they were kept were called barracks. He also found out that men in white coats were often veterinarians, that Friday was the day that mules at the Academy got molasses with their mash, that secretaries smelled pleasant and would often bring a mule a little something. Jackson also told him that the football season was still two months away.

"So we don't have much to do, really," Jackson

said. "Except to improve your mind and your self-image."

They started the lessons that very afternoon.

"We'll begin with A," Jackson suggested. "For Anatomy."

"Hooray," said Hemi. "Alphabetical order. I love things in alphabetical order."

Jackson began. "Ahem. Let us start by saying that the mule is a creature with an interesting and useful anatomy, or body. You might say that every part of a mule is designed for efficiency."

"Hey, I like your beginning," Hemi enthused.

"Please don't interrupt. It gets me confused."

Jackson continued. "As I was saying, the mule's anatomy is useful in every way. For instance, we have small hooves. This makes us surefooted, especially for going over mountains and other rough kinds of terrain."

"Hmmm," said Hemi, to show that he was concentrating on what Jackson was saying.

"Going from the feet to the head, one notes that we have large ears, which are a distinct plus, since as a result we have very acute hearing. It is said that you can talk to a horse, but you may chat and whisper to a mule. But that is by no means the end of our story. . . ."

"Oh, I should hope not," said Hemi, enthralled.

"Do *not* interrupt."

"Oh. Sorry."

"Another great trait of the mule is our strength.

Carefully loaded, a mule can carry three hundred to three hundred fifty pounds . . . and can travel with it up to twenty-five miles a day.

"A mule is stronger than its father, the donkey, or jackass, and smarter than its mother, the horse.

"But," said Jackson, warming to his climax, "the most remarkable trait of the mule . . . and I say this modestly," he added, looking hard at his audience of one, ". . . the most remarkable trait of the mule is its stamina. Mules almost never get tired, almost never get sick, and can be depended on to come through in spite of all handicaps, roadblocks, misfortunes, bad breaks, and calamities. All that a mule requires is to be treated with kindness and respect, to get clean water, and food that is fresh and crisp.

"To sum up," Jackson shouted in ringing tones, "the mule is a sensitive spirit in a robust body."

"Bravo, bravo," cried Hemi, quite carried away with the lesson.

"How's that for building your self-image?"

"Terrific. A-Number-One-Superfine."

"Well, now," said Jackson, quite exhausted by his lecture, "that's enough for one day. Tomorrow we'll go to H. History. We will discuss some of the historical episodes where mules have distinguished themselves. I think you'll like that."

"I'm sure I will. But what happened to B, C, D, E, F, and G?"

"If you're going to tell me how to teach this

course . . ." Jackson sounded offended.

"Oh. No. Not at all. I just meant . . ." Hemi was anxious not to hurt his new friend's feelings. "That's perfectly all right with me. Really."

The next day, true to Jackson's promise, they talked about History.

"You know, of course, that the mule is mentioned in the Bible."

Hemi hadn't known that.

"The famous Greek poet Homer knew of mules, and there is a line in the *Iliad* in which a mule is mentioned."

Hemi didn't know who Homer was and what the *Iliad* was, but he was afraid to interrupt to say so.

"And George Washington, the father of our country, was very partial to mules. He once ran an ad in the paper, offering his prize jackass to anyone who had a mare and who wanted to breed mules."

Hemi's self-image was improving every minute.

"Mules played a very important part in the Civil War. They carried supplies for both the North and the South. And in the great Indian Wars of the Southwest, mules were invaluable help to the U.S. Army.

"In fact," Jackson continued, "one mule pack train in the Indian Wars once covered two hundred eighty miles in three days."

"Why, that's better than ninety miles a day," said Hemi, who was excellent in Math.

"Quite right. And that is why the Army thinks so highly of mules. Which is why you and I are here today. We are here for old times' sake, in a manner of speaking."

Hemi thought longingly of the good old days. He wished that he had been alive then, when mules did great deeds.

"I wish there were a war on now," he cried eagerly. "I wish I could be a hero and carry supplies or pull the cannon or . . ."

"Bite your tongue," said Jackson sternly. "A lot of mules got killed in wars, including World War I. You should consider yourself lucky that they don't use us in wars anymore. Now machines do what we used to do."

Machines again. Hemi sighed. It seemed as if every time he turned around, a machine was replacing him.

"Maybe I shouldn't tell you any more. A little learning is a dangerous thing. You see, you are already becoming discontented."

"Oh, no. I'm not. Really. Please do go on."

Jackson did go on. That way the summer passed, and most of the alphabet. Hemi learned everything there was to know about mules.

The final lesson made a most profound impression on Hemi. One night, Jackson said to him, "We're about finished with this course. We're up to W. Wisdom."

"Oh, good," said Hemi. "Tell me something very wise."

"The wisest thing I know will make you sad."

"How can something wise make me sad?"

"Wisdom often is like that," said Jackson, frowning.

"Go ahead. I can manage it," said Hemi bravely.

"Well, here goes. What I want to tell you is this. . . . Do you know how babies are born?"

"Sure. We covered that under S. Sex Education. We did frogs, birds, bees, chickens, cows, et cetera. We even started to do where mules come from, but I told you that my father had already explained it to me."

"Yes. Well. The point is, a mule can be born, but . . . it can't . . ."

"Can't what?"

"Can't have babies. Reproduce. Give birth. We're sterile."

"We're what?"

"Sterile. Means we can't produce baby mules. Or baby anything else, for that matter. In other words," Jackson said gently, "no female mule can be a mother. And you will never be a father."

"In other words," said Hemi, "I'm the end of the line?"

"Exactly."

"Mother Nature!" Hemi shook his head unbelievingly. "Now that's a very queer feeling," he said. "To know that you'll never be the father of a family."

"I know," said Jackson.

"It's also lonely," said Hemi. "And quite sad."

Hemi was quiet for a long time.

He was thinking, as he did very often lately, of Melville. He wished Melville were here. He wondered if Melville knew about mules being sterile. Probably. He wished Melville could talk to him about it. He wished Melville could talk to him about a lot of things. Hemi sighed deeply.

"Well, I'll tell you one thing," he said finally to Jackson.

"What's that?"

"If you're the end of the line, then that's all the more reason to do something with your life. I'd better make the most of it. Like Mama said."

6   Army Life

And then it was football season. The leaves turned
color, and the chrysanthemums began to bud in the
suburban gardens. Down on the Academy football
field, helmeted cadets appeared. They ran around
and called to each other and rolled about on the
mushy ground.

"It does my heart good to see them at it again,"
Jackson said. "When football season comes around,
I feel that all's right with the world. I can't wait to
get out on that field," he said eagerly.

Hemi wanted to know what kind of field it was.
"Is it alfalfa? Chicory? Legumes of various sorts?"
His mouth watered to think of grazing on a delicious
football field.

Jackson soon set him straight about that.

"It's not an eating type field at all. It's a playing field."

"What do they play?"

"They have this ball made of pigskin and . . ."

"Pigskin?" said Hemi, shocked, thinking of all his friends from the farm who were pigs.

"They take this football and . . . they fight over it. One team tries to get it away from the other team, and carry it across this line. Sometimes they kick it past one another and sometimes they just try to run with it. The other team tries to catch them and knock them down."

"Doesn't it hurt?"

"Sometimes they do get hurt. Galbraith had a broken neck last year . . ."

"Well, why don't they just take turns with the ball?"

"Then there wouldn't be any game!"

"You mean they hurt themselves just for a game?"

Jackson looked annoyed. "I'm not going to talk to you about it anymore. You'll have to see for yourself."

On opening day, Army played a home game. Jackson was trotted out a few hours before the game and groomed until his coat shone. Then he was taken away and Hemi didn't see him for several hours. He had no idea what was happening, but from the pasture he could faintly hear the cheers and the sound of the Army band.

When Jackson was finally led in at dusk, he looked mighty pleased.

"We won," he said with satisfaction. "Thirteen–ten. Wczykowski kicked a field goal in the fourth quarter. Magnificent. And there was one punt formation that . . . But I guess you don't know what I'm talking about, eh, boy? Well, you'll see. Great. Great game. Wonderful spirit. Sport."

"I guess I'll get the hang of it," said Hemi, not at all sure that he would.

Jackson brayed thunderously. " 'Course you will. Army will make a man out of you. Well, now, I've put in a good day's work. Think I'll hit the hay."

He still hasn't told me what he does, Hemi mused, as he listened to Jackson snoring.

Hemi's turn came a few days later. One morning he was led to the back room of the stable. He was groomed and curried and had sweet-smelling-powder put on his coat. They dressed him in a blanket that had a big A on it. They festooned a bridle of leather and brass around his neck and even put little leather leggings on him.

Hemi felt a little silly.

"Is all this necessary?" he asked Jackson, who was supervising his getting dressed. "Can't I be a mascot without wearing this getup?"

"Nope. It's the Army way. Now just relax and follow orders and everything will be all right. You'll enjoy it."

"Tell me again what I do," Hemi said, nervously.

"When the band strikes up, you'll be led across the field. Then you stand quietly at attention while they play the National Anthem. Then you'll be led to the sidelines and you can watch the game. At the half, they'll march you out on the field again. And if Army wins, one of the cadets rides you. You get to lead the victory parade. It's all pageantry."

"What's pageantry?"

"It's something that makes people feel good."

Just then the groom came and led Hemi away.

When he walked out on the football field for the first time, Hemi could hardly believe his ears.

Between the band and the cheering, he was being bombarded with sound. It seemed to collect in his head until he was not at all sure that his poor skull wasn't about to burst. For a moment, all he could think of was running away. But then . . .

Steady, Hemi, he warned himself. Keep cool. You are here as a symbol of all the mules who ever did great deeds.

So, head held high, he marched across the football field. The cheering increased in volume, but Hemi couldn't tell whether they were cheering him, the football team, the band, or the United States Army in general. However, in case it was he, Hemionus, for whom the crowd cheered, he looked first to the right, then to the left, the way Jackson had shown him so many times.

He enjoyed the sensation that people might be cheering him, Hemionus. A mule. It's not bad, he

thought. In fact, it's very nice to be cheered. Even, he added, if you didn't do anything to deserve it. Well, he thought soberly, because he was a deep-thinking mule, not quite as nice as if you did.

Now he was led to the sidelines and the game began.

Hemi watched closely. He didn't understand the scoring and he couldn't quite figure out the plays, but he tried to find something in all of it that would give him the feelings that Jackson seemed to have for football. Toward the last half of the second quarter it began to rain, and in a few minutes the field was a sea of mud.

Hemi watched the players struggling in the wet.

"I suppose if you're willing to hold on to a ball no matter what, even if you get yourself all over mud, well, I suppose that's *something*," Hemi speculated. "But *what* is it? That's what I would like to know."

"It's grit. That's what it is. Pure grit," Jackson told him when Hemi got back to the barn. "That's what I've been trying to tell you. Didn't you get that old Army do-or-die spirit? Didn't our noble cadets impress you? Didn't you *feel* it?"

"I felt something, but I think it was a draft," said Hemi soberly. "Anyway, you were right about one thing. It's nothing like plowing."

After that, Hemionus and Jackson took turns going to the home games. And when the team played out of town, one or the other of them was put on a special Army train and sent to the game, along with a veterinarian and a groom.

Hemi enjoyed the traveling part. He liked seeing new places. But outside of that, he simply couldn't work up much enthusiasm for being an Army mule.

"I don't see why you don't like it," Jackson told him one day.

Hemi tried to explain. "Maybe it's the music. It's so loud. I don't really like marching music. I like Folk Rock, Rhythm and Blues . . . even a little Opera once in a while. But that oompa oompa . . ." He shook his head.

Jackson didn't understand a word of what Hemi was trying to say.

Another time, Hemi said, "There doesn't seem to be any *direction* to being an Army mule. The thing is, it doesn't *go* anywhere. Don't you feel you'd like some direction to your life, Jackson?"

"Direction?" said Jackson. "I know Gee for right and Haw for left. What other directions are there?"

"Why, there are lots of others. There's the other side of the mountain, and beyond the valley and past the next pasture. The world is full of directions. Don't you remember H, History of Mules? And Q, Quests of Mules? And Searches of Mules, under S?"

"I'd say you belong under W, for Weird Mules," said Jackson. "Here you are, picked by the Army to be a mascot. Many try but few are chosen, you know. You have a chance to live your whole life in comfort. Good food. Lots of time off. No getting obsolete. No getting sent to the Meat Packer. And what do you do? You toss it all aside for some crazy letter of the alphabet. I just don't understand you, Hemionus."

Hemi didn't quite understand it himself. He wished Melville were there. Hemi knew he'd understand.

When winter came, things went from bad to worse. Being an Army mascot became downright uncomfortable.

As he stood on the fifty-yard line on a sub-zero day, Hemi's thoughts were bitter.

I wouldn't mind so much if I were rescuing an explorer, lost in the wilderness. Or if I were carrying supplies to the soldiers in a great important battle. But just to be standing freezing on a *football* field with the wind whistling past your ears . . . it's downright silly, is what it is.

"Wasn't it great?" Jackson would ask when he came home. "Aren't you exhilarated from being out in the bracing air? Did we win?"

"I think I won a head cold," Hemi would say glumly.

The one thing that cheered Hemi was the thought of Christmas. "At Christmastime," he reasoned, "Melville will come home on vacation. He will go to Mr. Parkhurst's farm to say hello, and someone will tell him where I am. He will take the next train, I'm sure, and come to visit me. Loaded with presents in

54

every flavor. Molasses, chocolate . . . coffee almond. . . .

"We'll sit and talk. He'll sing a lot, and play his transistor radio. He'll know what I should do. He'll tell me if he thinks I ought to be an Army mule."

Hemi dreamed of Melville every night.

The Christmas holidays came. The garlands were hung, even over the stable.

The secretaries bought a little tree for the veterinarian's office adjoining the stable, and they trimmed it with tinsel and winking lights. The cadets came around to see the tree and the secretaries, and they brought apples and candy canes for Hemi and Jackson. Hemi liked the carols and the candy canes. But most of all he liked the fact that Melville was coming.

But the holidays came and went and Melville didn't come.

And then the Christmas decorations were down and Hemi knew in his heart that Melville wasn't coming. At first, he tried to figure out the reasons why.

"Maybe they didn't give him my right address.

"Maybe he missed his train.

"Maybe he got sick."

But, as always, the Why of it was troublesome. He thought and thought about it. One day he made up his mind.

"Jackson," he said firmly, "if Melville couldn't come to me, there is only one thing to do."

"What's that?" asked Jackson.

"I will have to go to him."

"You can't do that. You can't just leave the Army. That makes you a deserter."

"In that case," said Hemi, "I guess that's what I'll have to be."

7   Escape

Hemi was determined. But leaving the Academy was easier said than done. Even if Hemi managed to get out of the barn without being seen, there were sentries and patrols and security M.P.'s everywhere.

"The thing to do is to keep your eyes open," Hemi said to himself. "Be ready when opportunity knocks."

Opportunity came a week later, on the day of the traditional Army-Navy Game.

"You're so lucky to be going," said Jackson. "It isn't every mule who gets a chance to see an Army-Navy Game."

"Whoopee," said Hemi morosely, as he was led away.

Hemi spent the first part of the game trying to

shut out the sounds of the band and to forget that his ears were freezing. At the half he was walked around the field a bit. That warmed him up and he paid more attention to the second half of the game. And it was in the final minutes, with the score tied at 3–3, that Hemi glanced at the scoreboard and got his perfect idea.

If you want to sneak away from somewhere, he thought, the best time to do it is when everyone is thinking about something else. Because then they won't be thinking about you. Which is what may happen in a few minutes in this football game.

Hemi began to watch the game with intense concentration. He had a personal stake in the outcome of this game, and that gave it a distinctly interesting flavor.

"Come on, Army," he muttered through clenched teeth. "Get in there and fight."

He monitored every play. "How about an end run," he suggested when there were five minutes left to play.

"I'll settle for a field goal," he murmured at two minutes.

Forty-five seconds before the final whistle, Army got the ball and Cadet Alvin Todhunter ran around the end that brought him right in front of where Hemi was standing. Two burly Navy linemen headed straight for him. In an agony of anxiety, Hemi yelled, "Watch out, Todhunter." His sharp bray cut through the crowd's shouting. The two

Navy linemen heard it. For a split second, they both turned in astonishment at the loud and commanding sound coming from the mule. Given that split second, Todhunter sprinted through Navy's line on a spectacular run that took the ball for a touchdown.

The whistle blew. That was it. 9–3, favor of Army.

In the midst of the band playing, the people screaming, the players clapping each other on the back, the hats in the air, the hubbub . . . and just before the victory march that he was to have led, Hemionus walked quietly out of the stadium.

By the time they missed him, he had slipped down a side street and was trotting purposefully toward the turnpike.

"The first thing I'd better do is get rid of this blanket," he said to himself. "Makes me stand out like a sore thumb." He shook it off.

The bridle and bit was not as easy to get rid of. After a few experimental shakes, he tried to rub it off against a door. Then he tried to spit the bit out of his mouth. That didn't work, either. I guess I'll just have to live with the bridle and bit, he reasoned, and without any further hesitation, he continued on his way.

Fortunately, it was a holiday, and the streets were deserted. The few people who were out looked up when they heard the jingling of his bridle, but, while they were startled to see a mule on the streets, they didn't do anything about it. They thought that someone might be playing a practical joke on someone.

So Hemi got through the city without incident.

It was dusk by the time he got to the highway. He surveyed the signposts—East, South, North, West.

"West is where Melville said he was going," he reminded himself, "so that's where I'll go."

He had no doubt that, once in the West, he would find Melville.

He followed the arrows which pointed in a westerly direction, and after a brief moment of confusion at the traffic circle, he found himself trotting along Highway 65, headed west. He kept up a steady pace, making sure that he was well over to the side of the road and not out in full view on the highway.

"I'm sure they've discovered by now that I'm missing," he mused. "There'll be an all-points alarm out for me. I'm a deserter, is what I am." He wondered what the Army did to deserters. Whatever it was, he was anxious to avoid it if possible.

He amused himself for a while by drilling Army style. "Hup two three four, hup two three four." The miles went by. Then for the next hour, he did some deep thinking about Whys and Wherefores.

Now he noticed that it was quite dark. At about the same time, he realized that he was hungry.

Hemi looked around for something to nibble on. He spied a clump of weeds growing alongside the highway and ambled over to them. He took a few

experimental nibbles, as best he could with the bit in his mouth.

"Pheugh!" He spit them out hastily. "They taste like what cars smell like. Rule number one for runaway mules: Don't eat the weeds from the side of the highway."

Hemi moved farther away from the road and went up a little hill. There he found a patch of grass and sweet clover that tasted familiar. When he'd finished eating, he felt a lot more cheerful.

At my present pace, he thought with satisfaction, I will have traveled twenty miles by morning.

"I feel good," he mused. "I feel free and searching and full of hope. That is the way a mule should feel."

He thought of Jackson, snoring peacefully back at the Academy stable. "He'll never know what it's like to be free, and searching. But he likes being an Army mule. If he likes it, that's fine. To each his own." Hemi felt sorry he hadn't had a chance to say good-bye to Jackson.

Now the steady sound of his own hooves clomping along the shoulder of the highway and the whizzing sound of the cars going by were beginning to make Hemi sleepy.

"Think I'll catch forty winks," he decided. He looked for a spot and found one, in a little valley behind a ridge, far enough off the highway so that no one could possibly see him. He had no trouble falling asleep.

Hemi awoke at dawn. After washing his face in a brook and taking a long drink of cool water, he was ready to start again. He walked to the top of the ridge and stood there for a moment, surveying the morning with pleasure and anticipation. His silhouette was clearly visible from the highway, but for the moment, Hemi wasn't thinking about that. He was thinking about pink sunrises and the smell of freedom.

He didn't see the old pickup truck slow down and pull off the highway below where he was standing. He came down the ridge slowly. and started to trot along in the grass. Now he saw the truck. It appeared to be empty.

An empty truck, he thought. I wonder where the owner is? Maybe he left the highway to pick flowers. Or to watch the sunrise. Or maybe he's answering a call of nature.

At that very moment, the man who was standing in back of the pickup truck was reaching for a long rope.

Hemi trotted on, oblivious. This is the finest day of my life, he thought. I am young and free and making the most of it. My mother would be proud of me if she could see me now.

He felt something slide over his head and around his neck.

Hemi started to run as fast as he could. For a few brief moments, he seemed to be outrunning whatever it was that had hold of him. But then he felt the rope tighten. He turned around and saw that the rope was attached to the truck. A man stepped out from behind the truck. Before he realized what was happening, the Man had roped Hemi tightly, dragged him up the ramp, and shoved him in the back of the truck.

There was no way out.

"Good-bye, freedom," Hemionus mourned. "You sure didn't last very long."

8 Captured

It's not easy to be standing up in the back of a pickup truck when the pickup truck is barreling along a highway. Every time it took a curve, Hemi had to brace his four feet firmly and lean in the direction in which the truck was turning. Every time the truck stopped, he had to brace his forelegs and lean backwards. It was only after he had mastered both of these maneuvers that he dared to concentrate on the Man who had captured him.

Hemi didn't much like what he saw.

What he saw was the back of a sweat-stained jacket. Coming out of the collar of the jacket was a fat, red, freckled neck. Topping it all was a large head of greasy brown hair with one bald spot in the

65

back, through which a dirty scalp showed.

The whole effect was not encouraging.

However, Hemi thought, let's not be unfair. Let's not judge a person by the back of his neck or the greasiness of his hair. Or by any other single part of him, for that matter, he added. The whole Man, taken in total, may be A-Number-One for all we know.

"A-Number-One," he repeated, to cheer himself up.

Meanwhile, the pickup truck was rattling along the road. It was going over hills and passing farms and gas stations and general stores. After a while there began to be a new look to the countryside. The air was softer; the trees were unfamiliar.

Hemi sensed that he was far from the city he'd walked through just the day before.

At noon, the Man drove into a parking place near a truck stop. Hemi guessed that it was lunchtime.

He waited hopefully. The Man went into the diner and was gone for a long time. When he came out he was chewing on a toothpick. Without a word to Hemi, he climbed into the truck and they started off again.

"Hey!" Hemi was hungry. He was also thirsty. Maybe I have slipped his mind, he thought. I'd better remind him that I am here.

"Ahem!" he called, braying loudly. Then again, even louder, "Ahem."

No answer. He looked at the back of the Man's

neck. It showed no sign that the Man had understood.

By this time it was mid-afternoon. The sun beat down on the open truck. Hemi was tired and hot, and he was having more and more trouble keeping his balance when the truck went around curves. But the Man never even glanced in his rearview mirror to see if his captive was still right side up.

At eight o'clock that night, the truck stopped. The Man opened the back.

"Okay, Henry. Git a move on."

Who is he talking to? Hemi wondered.

"You! Henry! Git!"

Hemi finally got the idea. Why, he means me, he realized.

Before he could respond to the Man's direction, Hemi felt a terrible pressure on his neck.

"There's no need to do that to my neck," he protested.

The Man yanked him out of the truck and took him over to a trough, where he slopped some hay and water at him. By this time, Hemi was so tired and upset that he could hardly eat. He drank a little water and staggered back to the truck.

More driving. At least, Hemi thought to himself, it's cooler at night. He watched the moon rise and tried to keep his mind off his troubles.

Many hours later, they stopped in front of a ramshackle house which stood at the edge of a swamp. Hemi had never seen a swamp before. He shivered a little as he looked at the twisted, moss-covered trees hanging spookily over the black water. "This must surely be Parts Unknown," he decided. "Maybe I'll meet Papa here."

The thought of his father brought a lump to his throat. What would Papa say if he could see him now? Or Mama?

Or Melville, who didn't even know that Hemi was trying to find him.

Now he felt the pressure on his neck again. The Man forced him to get out of the truck. He gave him food and water in the same careless way.

While Hemi was eating, a thin-lipped woman in a bathrobe came out of the house.

"Where'd ya get the mule?" she asked sullenly.

"Found him wandering around down by Highway 65. Musta got away from som'un." The man chuckled. "Finders keepers."

"Hmph. It'll probably cost more to feed him than he's worth."

"Don't worry. I'll make him earn his keep. And he ain't gonna get too durn much to eat. Jest enough to keep him workin'."

Hemi had now made up his mind about one thing. He didn't like the Man. He is as mean as the back of his neck would lead you to believe, he decided.

The Man took Hemi's Army bit and bridle off and gave it to the woman. "Put this away," he said. "We'll take it into town and see how much we can get for it."

Now the Man led Hemi, none too gently, to a drafty little shack in back of the house. Without another word, he shoved him in, put up the latch, and left him there.

Hemi looked around at his new home. He saw the rotting boards, the dirt on the floor, the pile of beer cans in the corner. He saw the holes in the roof where the moon shone in and made scary shadows on the wall.

He shivered.

"Can this be Parts Unknown?" he asked himself. "A drafty barn filled with rusty cans?"

He thought longingly of his first home in the Parkhursts' clean barn. Then he thought of his second home at the Academy, with Jackson, his friend and teacher. Why had he wanted to leave? Wherever he had been before was certainly better than where he was now. He shook his head.

"The moral of the story is—when you try to make your life better, there is always the chance that you'll make it worse."

He looked up through a hole in the roof. He could just catch a glimpse of the sky. And freedom.

Mournfully, Hemi said, "Melville, wherever you are, do you know what kind of song I would sing tonight, if I could sing?"

He imagined Melville saying, "No, man, what kind of song would you sing?"

And Hemi whispered to the night, "The Blues, man. I would sing the Blues."

9 Hard Times

The next day, just as Hemi's stomach was beginning to settle down after the truck ride, the Man appeared, carrying a crude bit and halter.

He stepped into Hemi's stall. With one quick motion, he shoved the bit into Hemi's mouth and threw the leather strap over his head.

Hemi hated the way he did it. When the Man pulled on the halter, the metal bit pressed against the inside of his mouth where the flesh was tender and soft.

The Man kept on pulling.

The more he pulled, the more it hurt.

The more it hurt, the more Hemi didn't move.

The pain confused him; he didn't know what the Man wanted him to do.

The more Hemi stood still, the madder the Man got.

"So. You're going to be stubborn, are you?" the Man snarled. He hit Hemi with the leather strap.

It didn't really hurt all that much; Hemi had a tough hide. It was more that he was puzzled that anyone would strike him. He had never been hit before in his whole mule life. He didn't know what it meant. He also didn't know what the Man meant by stubborn. What was stubborn? Where had he heard that word before?

Before the day was over, Hemionus learned a lot of new things. And none of them was pleasant.

He discovered that working for the Man meant being loaded down with a weight heavy enough for *two* mules, then forced to carry it long distances. It meant being given no water the whole day. And if he faltered or stopped for a moment, the Man hit him.

By evening Hemi could barely stand on his legs. And then, to top off a miserable day, when he got his feed it was moldy.

That night, back in his shack, Hemi took stock of the situation.

He decided that he was in bad trouble.

"The way I figure it," he said to himself wearily, "this Man is going to work me to death."

72

What to do about it? That was the question. Should he make the best of it, put up with the long hours and short rations, and hope that things would improve?

As he thought about it, he remembered something out of his childhood. He remembered his father saying to him, "Don't be put upon."

Of course. That was it. That was what was happening. He was definitely being put upon. And what had his father advised? "Be stubborn."

Now, at last, Hemi understood what stubborn meant.

"I will be stubborn," he vowed. "As stubborn as a mule can be."

The following morning, when the Man walked into Hemi's stall, Hemi was ready for him. He took aim and let fly with his back legs.

"Considering that it is the first time in my whole life that I ever kicked someone, that was really a pretty A-Number-One kick," Hemi reflected, as he looked down at the figure sprawled on the floor. "I think Jackson would be proud of me."

The Man beat him for it, but Hemi considered it worth it. After he got tired of beating him, the Man loaded Hemi up with about 700 pounds of cordwood, and tried to get him to carry it to the shed. But Hemi was not about to oblige him. When the load had exceeded what he thought was a reasonable weight, Hemi sat down in the dirt. No amount of swearing,

kicking, and hitting could persuade him to get up.

After a while, the Man went away. I won that one, Hemi thought proudly.

But the Man was back all too soon. This time, he was carrying a big stick.

He raised it to hit Hemi.

Hemi promptly bit him on the knee.

The Man howled and disappeared into his house, limping.

I think I won that one, too, Hemi thought, pleased at the results that stubbornness was producing.

But the Man was by no means finished with punishments.

There was no dinner for Hemi that night.

The next morning, the Man tied Hemi to a post in the yard and left him there.

He didn't feed him for two days.

Hemi spent the first day thinking about what he would do with his life if he ever got away. He spent the second day thinking about food. He thought of juicy fields of clover, in full flower. He dreamed of alfalfa and jewelweed, washed down with a snack of sassafras leaves. He fantasized food—fields of food, *mountains* of food. He got hungrier and hungrier. His dreams of food got simpler. Just a pail of oats. That's what I would dearly love. Plain oats. If it could have a little molasses mixed in with it, it would be ever so nice. But it doesn't have to, he added hastily. He dozed, dreaming of oats and molasses.

By the morning of the third day, Hemi was feeling faint. He had eaten every blade of grass around him and was hungrily contemplating some papers that were lying around the yard.

Just as he thought he couldn't stand it one more second, the Man came with some food.

"You ought to be sobered up a bit," he said. "Mebbe now you'll be ready to do as you're told. . . ."

He stepped into Hemi's range to put the harness on him. He ducked just in time to avoid a pair of flying hooves.

Now the Man was really angry. He took away Hemi's water.

Of all the meanness to which a mule can be subjected, this is the most painful.

This is not among the better things that can

happen to a mule, Hemi thought, after a day of thirst.

But he still wouldn't give in.

A mule is a sensitive spirit in a robust body, he told himself weakly. *We will not be put upon.*

That evening, the Man's wife asked him, "Ain't you got that mule broke yet?"

"Never you mind," he snapped. The Man didn't like to be reminded of his failure.

"Must be a pretty ornery critter. Whyn't ya sell him?"

"I couldn't get a plugged nickel for him. Nobody'd want him. Who wants a mule that won't do a lick of work?"

"I know someone'll give us money fer him," the Woman said slyly.

"Who's that?"

"The Meat Packer over ta Lynchburg."

The Man looked pleased.

"Hey, woman, that is one fine idea. I'll sell the varmint to the Meat Packer. Serve him right, too. Good fer nothin'."

"Better keep him fer a few more days, though. Fatten him up a little. He looked half-dead when I seen him last."

"Yeah. I'll go feed and water him now." The man grinned until his rotted teeth showed. "Wouldn't want anything to happen to him."

Hemi could barely stand up when the Man showed up with the food and water. He drank first. Then, as he felt his strength coming back, he ate. By the time he had finished and was back in his stall, he felt considerably better.

"Maybe the Man has had a change of heart," he speculated. "Maybe he's decided to be nice to me. Well—that's good. I'm certainly not one to hold a grudge. If he's nice to me, I'll work for him. That's fair. I'll work until I pay for my keep, then I'll go find Melville."

He was interrupted by a thin, piping voice. "I wouldn't make any deals, if I were you."

10 *A Snake Speaks*

"Who's that?" asked Hemi, startled.

"It's me. Corn Snake."

"Snake!" Hemi was startled. "I've always been afraid of snakes."

"That's why I may not come out. Or if I do I shall take my time about it. So you can get used to the idea."

Hemi was uneasy at the idea that there was a snake in his shed and he hadn't even known it.

"What are you doing here?" he asked. "Have you been here long?"

"A lot longer than you have. I've lived here all my life."

"Well, why didn't you say something before this?"

"No reason to. Besides," Corn Snake added, "we don't like to call attention to ourselves. A snake doesn't particularly enjoy having another creature go into conniption fits as soon as the word snake is mentioned. It isn't all that pleasant. So we just keep to ourselves."

Something about this statement touched Hemi, who was, after all, a kindhearted, sensitive mule. Suddenly, he felt very warmly disposed toward the snake.

"Oh, I do wish you'd come out. I'd like to see you. I promise not to have a conniption fit."

"In that case, I will," said Corn Snake.

A moment later, Hemi saw a movement in the corner where the tin cans were. Slowly, a small shape separated itself from the shadows.

Corn Snake was quite beautiful. Her body was a warm tan color, and along her back was a pattern of crimson blotches, bordered with black. She came toward him, stopped, and curled up at his feet.

"Here I am," she said. "*Elaphe guttata*. Otherwise known as Corn Snake. At your service."

Hemi was pleasantly surprised.

"Why, you're very attractive. I thought—I mean —no offense but—I thought you'd be ugly and slimy."

"That's what they all think," said the snake impatiently. "If people would only take the trouble to check the facts, they'd find out. But do they? No. It's so tiresome. So they say we're slimy. And sneaky. And that we milk cows, and I don't know what else.

"When, as a matter of fact," she said, "we are quite beneficial. For instance, you would have been up to your ears in rats if it weren't for me. As it is, have you seen a rat or mouse all the time you've been living in this stall?"

Hemi had to admit that he hadn't.

"Certainly not. Because I have been doing my job. I have been ridding this place of rodents *and* eating well. Si-mul-tan-eously," she said with satisfaction.

"Well, I appreciate it," said Hemi. "But how come you decided to show up now?"

"Because I want to give you some good advice."

"I'm all ears," said Hemi. "Go ahead."

The little snake uncurled a bit and began to speak earnestly.

"You think that the Man has had a change of heart. You think he means to be decent to you from now on. Don't kid yourself. I happen to know that at this very moment he and that horrible wife of his are talking about selling you to the Meat Packer and figuring out just how much you are worth to them in the can."

"Oh! No! Not again!" The hair on the back of Hemi's neck stood straight up.

"A word to the wise is sufficient. You'd better do something."

"I know I've got to get out of here," Hemi said desperately. "But how? The stall is always locked. There's no way. At least I can't seem to think of one."

"Never mind," said Corn Snake soothingly, "we have a few days to think about it, while they fatten you up. I'd advise you to get a lot of rest and try not to worry. While you're doing that I'll think of a plan."

She was gone as quickly and as quietly as she had come.

The stall suddenly seemed very empty without the friendly snake.

"Snake. Are you there, Snake?" Hemi whispered into the darkness.

He heard her small, hissing voice.

"I'm right here behind the oil drum. Go to ssssleep," she replied.

True to Corn Snake's prediction, the Man spent the next few days being extraordinarily good to Hemionus. He fed him fresh mash twice a day, and the water, Hemi noticed, came from the spring. Hemi began to regain his strength.

Each morning after the Man had fed him and gone away, Corn Snake would appear. She would curl up at Hemi's feet in a shaft of sunlight, and the two of them would talk.

Hemi told Snake all about Melville and his singing and about how he was going to find Melville and why. Corn Snake didn't seem to have any trouble understanding about looking for a direction to your life.

"In your place I would do exactly the same thing," she told him emphatically.

The more he talked to her, the more Hemi liked Corn Snake. After a while he couldn't believe that he had ever disliked snakes.

And then came the morning of the fourth day.

Corn Snake was late. At last she appeared, looking extremely cheerful.

"How are you this morning, Hemi?"

"Worried," he confessed. "I'm sure today's the day. In fact, I didn't close my eyes all night."

"I never close my eyes," said the snake. "But of course my eyelids are transparent, so I don't have to. However, this is no time for chit-chat about my anatomy. I've come to tell you that I have a plan."

She outlined her plan to Hemi. When she'd finished, Hemi said, "Are you sure it will work?"

"Positive," she said. "If there's anything I know, it's how people act with snakes. It will happen as I said, I guarantee. And, even if it doesn't, you can't be any worse off than you are now."

"All right, I'll do it," said Hemi. "I've got to take the chance."

"He'll be here in a little while to feed you. Let's go over it one more time." They went over their plan, step by step.

"Remember," she advised, "if you make it, head for the swamp. He can't follow you through there. Once you're in the swamp stay close to the stream and keep the sun at your back. After a while, you should come to the road that leads to the highway. Then it's westward ho! again for you, and you'll be in the clear. By the by, when you're in the swamp, don't get your hooves stuck in the muck." She looked pleased. "Why, that's practically poetry!"

Corn Snake put her head down and held her whole body to the ground. "Oops, I feel his vibrations. He's coming. Let's say good-bye now because I won't see you afterward. Good luck!"

"So long. I don't know how I can ever thank you enough," Hemi whispered.

"Just ssssay a good word for sssssnakes whenever you get the chance," she whispered, as she took her place in a dark corner.

The Man approached the shack, carrying a pail of water and a sack of feed and smiling broadly. He was thinking of the money he was going to make on Hemi's carcass. Now he pushed up the bar on the door and walked inside, leaving the door swinging open behind him. He went over to the stall. He opened the gate of the stall and . . . there, curled up on the floor, was . . .

"A snake!" he yelled. In the dim light, he couldn't see what kind of snake it was.

He backed away carefully. He put the food and water down slowly. Then he turned.

"Ugh! How I hate snakes," he muttered. "Gotta find something ta kill that snake. . . . Ah, this'll do," he said, as he took a rake off the wall.

Armed with the rake, the Man turned around— just in time to see Hemi going out the open door.

Corn Snake's plan had worked.

The Man raced out of the shack, furious at the thought of the mule getting away. He ran to the house to get his shotgun, shouting, "I'll shoot it. I'll shoot the varmint."

But by the time he'd located his gun and come outside again, the mule had been swallowed up by the thick tangle of trees that surrounded the swamp.

Hemi plunged into the semidarkness gratefully. He felt the early morning mist of the swamp close in around him, and the black water ripple around his hooves, covering his tracks.

He moved quietly through the shallow water, trying hard to make as little noise as possible. Every once in a while, he stopped and listened for sounds of pursuit. But the Man had given up; he was afraid to go into the swamp.

For the whole morning, Hemi made his way

through the Great Swamp. At first, though he heard rustling and plopping and birdcalls, the creatures of the swamp kept out of his way. But after a while, they seemed to sense that he wasn't an enemy, and began to show themselves. Frogs began to pop up on lily pads in front of him. Turtles scrambled up on logs to watch him go by. Water turkeys sitting in the sun with their wings spread to dry nodded to him as he passed. Dragonflies and other insects flew back and forth over his head, keeping him company as he walked. He nibbled a water hyacinth or two, and found them tasty.

"Actually," Hemi said to himself, "a swamp is not an unfriendly place at all. Once you get to know it, it's really quite nice. Sort of like a pasture, if the pasture was under water."

"It just goes to show you," he said, squinting up at the sun to get his bearings, "there were two things I didn't know anything about—corn snakes and swamps. I was afraid of both of them. And now," he added with satisfaction, "that I know them—I like them both. And I am not afraid."

So saying, he stepped out of the swamp and onto the road that Corn Snake had told him to watch for.

He stamped the mud off his hooves. "I wonder if Melville likes swamps," he said.

11 *Hard Travelin'*

Hemi didn't know exactly where he was going. But he knew that he wanted to get as far away as possible from where he'd been. And, above all, he wanted to find Melville.

"If I can just find Melville," he reasoned, "he'll understand everything. He'll even understand about the Search, under S. Because he's searching, too. We can do it together. Two heads will definitely be better than one for that kind of Search. Yes," Hemi concluded, "everything will be all right if only I can find Melville."

He was also determined to avoid being captured again. So he decided to stay away from major highways altogether, and to follow the little back roads. "On weekends," he told himself, "I will travel only at night. I will hide and sleep during the day."

Hemi began to work his way westward. Through Tennessee. Across Arkansas and Oklahoma. Across the top of Texas and the middle of New Mexico.

It was a long haul. And a lot of things happened. Once Hemi met a friendly herd of deer, and he traveled with them for a while. Another time he met an unfriendly Doberman, and he got away from him as quickly as possible. In one town an old lady hit him with an umbrella. In another a young man gave him a whole feedbag full of good oats. Sometimes he was warm in a green valley. Other times he was shivering with cold on a mountaintop. He was patted by children and scared by motorcycles. Still he went on. Through towns with names from storybooks—Tucumcari, Enchanted Mesa, Blue Water Lake. . . .

The miles passed. The months passed.

Hemi began to look altogether different. His coat got shaggy and his hooves were toughened from the long weeks of walking. You could hardly see the white star-shaped mark on his leg. His appearance began to suggest some creature of the wilds. Rough. Tough. Not to be tampered with.

"A wild mule," people who saw him were apt to say. "No telling what he'll do. Best thing is to keep out of his way."

Once a group of cowboys on horseback tried to rope him, but he was used to dodging danger by now, and he hid in an abandoned garage until they went yipping by. Then he hightailed it for the woods and continued his journey. Once he was even chased by a helicopter, but he hid in a canyon.

Mostly, people kept out of his way. And vice versa.

It took Hemionus over a year to travel across the United States. But, at last, he reached Arizona. It was late May when he arrived, and the desert was in bloom.

"I couldn't have got here at a better time," he told himself with satisfaction, surveying the scenery from the top of a red rock mesa. "The desert in bloom is a never-to-be-forgotten sight."

How many mules, he thought wonderingly, have seen what I've seen, have tasted pasture plants and swamp plants and have also nibbled little alpine plants from the tops of mountains? How many mules have seen a desert sunset and the sun coming up over the Great Smokies?

Dazzled by the sunset, and by the fact that he was coming to the end of his long journey, Hemi scampered into the desert like a young foal. He ran round and round, kicking up his heels and rolling in the sand. If anyone had seen him at that particular moment, they would have said, "There is a mule that has a burr under its tail." Or, "There is a mule that has a bee in its ear." But neither of these speculations would have been true. It was just that, for the moment, a mule named Hemi was happy. He had something to look back on and something to look forward to.

That night, as he stood under the star-studded sky, Hemi tried to imagine what it would be like to see Melville again.

He will be very glad to see me again, I know that, he thought. Even though it will be a great surprise to him that I am here when I should be there. Melville will scratch me in all the right places, I'm sure of that. He will tell me all about Agricultural School and talk to me of Botany and all those other things that he has been learning. We will make plans.

He wondered what sort of goodies Melville was keeping in his pockets these days, for special occasions. Did he still keep an Oh Henry bar in his shirt pocket, Hemi wondered.

Yes, he decided. He will definitely have an Oh Henry bar. And maybe a Milky Way, too. He may give me both of them. Yes, he reflected, this may well be a two-candy-bar occasion.

On that happy note, Hemi fell asleep.

The next morning he awoke hopeful and hungry.

"In another few hours, I will be face-to-face with my friend Melville," he told himself.

With his mind on the distance to Tucson, Hemi didn't give his full attention to selecting his breakfast. He simply reached for the green bushy plant that was at his feet, and didn't bother about looking it over before he nibbled.

This proved to be an almost fatal mistake. No one could have said that it was entirely his fault. Mules do eat prickly things. Hemi may have thought that a cactus was similar to a thistle, and therefore digestible. He must not have realized just how prickly a cactus can be.

His first bite made Hemi leap back. He spit out the large piece he'd bitten off the cactus plant. Too late. He had a mouthful of sharp cactus spines.

For a moment, Hemi was too surprised by the pain to do anything. He just stood there, hurting. In that one bite, he'd gotten spines in his lips and tongue, as well as on the inside of his mouth.

He shook his head vigorously, hoping to shake them off. It didn't work.

Almost immediately, his mouth began to throb painfully.

I'd better get to the Agricultural College as fast as I can and find Melville, he decided. Melville will take care of everything, including getting these spines out of my mouth. And the sooner, the better.

He moved across the desert, looking for signs that would tell him the way to Tucson. After about a half hour, he began to notice, at intervals, small, neat signposts. A345 said one, then the next said A346. And so on. Not long after the signs started, Hemi saw a large brown-and-white Hereford steer, standing alone in the field, grazing. He decided to ask him the way.

Hemi was careful to approach the bull from the front, in case Hereford steers do not like to be sneaked up on, the way mules don't. But the steer seemed very friendly. In fact, he seemed delighted to see Hemi.

"Excuse me," Hemi said politely, "do you happen to know the way to the Agricultural College?"

"You're standing on part of it," the steer answered in his deep voice. "This is the Experimental Desert Acreage."

"Oh," said Hemi. "That's fine. I . . ."

"Matter of fact," the bull continued, "I'm part of the experiment. It's in the Plant Management course. They're trying to see which plants I manage to eat."

"That's very interesting," said Hemi, speaking slowly because his mouth hurt so. "Well, I'll be on my way and I surely do appreciate . . ."

"Speaking of eating plants," said the steer, "you certainly did get a mouthful, didn't you? That's a real shame. Getting a snootful of cactus spines can make you feel really sick. I know. . . ."

"Yes, well, that's why I have to get going. My friend, he's going to . . ."

Hemi was anxious to leave, but the steer continued talking as if he hadn't heard him.

"The thing to do is not to eat the big ones. Look for the little juicy ones that don't have spines yet."

"Yes. Well . . . I'll certainly do that next time. Now if you'll excuse me I . . ."

"There's nothing tastier than a young cactus that doesn't have spines. You take the saguaro, for instance. You won't find a more tender . . ."

"I really *must* be going," said Hemi, who was feeling worse by the minute. "I am sorry. Maybe on the way back we could stop and . . ."

The Hereford finally understood.

"That's all right," he said sadly. "You run along. Just that I've been out here all alone for so long, I . . . well, you know. . . . Glad to have someone to talk to. . . . Now you just go straight down this road and you'll see the entrance to the college. Can't miss it.

"I hope you will come back," he called after Hemi. "I'll show you around A345. I know every inch of this turf."

Hemi promised he would, and left. When he looked back, the Hereford was looking at him with the saddest expression in his brown eyes. Hemi felt sorry for the loneliness of the Hereford steer. But he had a few other things on his mind.

Hemi arrived at the college around noon. He walked up to the door of the Administration building, under a burning sun, with an aching mouth full of cactus spines, only to read a sign which said:

"CLOSED FOR SUMMER VACATION. REGULAR CLASSES RESUME SEPTEMBER 1. ALL INQUIRIES SHOULD BE DIRECTED TO THE REGISTRAR. STUDENTS INVOLVED IN THE GRAND CANYON SUMMER PROJECT . . ."

Hemi didn't read any further.

Mother Nature! He had forgotten all about summer vacations!

He couldn't quite believe it, even when he thought more about it. Melville was probably back East for the summer, and might even at this very moment be asking Mr. Parkhurst where he, Hemi, was. While he, Hemi, was here in the West, looking for Melville.

"It ith thoo ironic. I don' think I can thtand it," he said, talking with difficulty because of his swollen tongue.

Now what? was his next thought. He knew that the first thing he must do was to get the spines out. He had learned early from his mother to take care of his mouth. Stands to reason, he thought now. No mouth, no eat. No eat . . . He wasn't anxious to complete that thought.

Hemi knew that he needed a human to help him, someone who could recognize what was wrong with him. So he headed for the nearest town. Once there, he trotted down the main street with his mouth open, hoping that someone would sense his problem.

Unfortunately, a drooling mule with his mouth open is liable to be mistaken for a dangerous, rabid mule, except by someone who knows both mules and cactus spines. There didn't seem to be anyone like that in this town. The first thing Hemi knew, people began to chase him, shouting "Crazy mule. Crazy mule." Poor Hemi was forced to turn on his heels and get out of town and back to the desert as fast as he could. Once he was safe, he decided that the best thing to do was to rest awhile.

He found a patch of shade made by an arch of rock, and closed his eyes. Just for a minute, he promised himself. Forty winks.

When he awoke, it was late afternoon. His mouth felt like it was on fire. His whole body felt weak, and he was shaking. He needed water. Badly. But there was no water in sight, and even Hemi, as full of stamina as he was, didn't have the strength to get up and find some.

He was in bad shape.

For the first time, Hemi realized the seriousness of his predicament.

Is it possible, he thought, that I will have to give up? After all this time, and all these thousands of miles, all my narrow escapes and my stamina and stick-to-it-iveness—after all this, is it possible that I shall be done in by a plant?

Now he could think only little pieces of thoughts. No one . . . will ever know . . . what happened to me . . . someday. . . .

He slept a little, and dreamed that he put up a sign over his whitened bones which said "It was me."

He awoke, delirious, with a new thought. At least if I had ended up in the dog dish . . . at least . . . I would have been a meal for something . . . but now. I'm wasted. . . . And I never had a chance to see Melville again . . . dear Melville. . . . "Goodbye, Melville," he sighed, his voice trailing off.

12 *Dancing Eyes*

Much, much later, Hemi dreamed that someone was bending over him and saying,

"Oh—the poor thing."

Then, in his dream, the hot sun, which had been beating down on him mercilessly, seemed to go behind a cloud. In the haze of his pain and fever, he thought, I am dreaming. I am dreaming and in my dream this creature whose voice I think I hear has made the sun go away. He was grateful that the creature had arranged it, even if it was only a dream.

Hemi thought that if it were not such a stupendous effort to open his eyes, he would check it out to see if he was dreaming.

Then Hemi felt his throbbing head being lifted

and put on something soft. Like a lap, he thought. Very much like a lap. Now a cool hand seemed to be touching his sore mouth and something was poured onto his lips. Whatever it was took away all pain in that area. And that was good.

He began to feel the cactus spines being gently pulled out of his lips, and then out of his tongue.

Still he didn't open his eyes. This is an A-Number-One-Superfine dream, Hemi thought to himself. No sense in waking up too soon.

The spines seemed to continue to be pulled out of his mouth. It was such a relief that his eyes watered.

"There, there," the voice of his dream said. "Don't cry. Only a few more."

Hemi's eyes continued to water. It's amazing how real a dream can be, Hemi thought. I seem to feel the tears running down my coat.

Moments later something unbelievably soft and cold filled his mouth and ran over his face. It felt like . . . like . . . Once, I remember, Melville gave me half of a soft ice-cream cone, Hemi thought. It felt just like this when it was in my mouth.

That was it. He was dreaming of a soft ice-cream cone.

Maybe it's not a dream, Hemi speculated. Maybe I'm dead and I'm in those great Green Pastures in the Sky. He thought maybe he would make the effort and open his eyes to see what Green Pastures looked like. But he was too tired.

Hemi slept.

When he awoke, it was dusk. He opened his eyes and looked straight up. Instead of seeing clouds, as he had expected, what he saw was an Indian blanket, right above his head. He frowned, puzzled. Could it be that in Green Pastures the clouds looked like Indian blankets?

Noting that keeping his eyes open wasn't too bad, Hemi stopped looking up and began to look around. It seemed clear, once he'd taken a good look, that not only was he alive, but he was lying comfortably in the desert in the cool of evening under an Indian blanket which was supported by four poles to make a kind of roof over him. Nor was he alone. A small girl with black braids was sitting nearby with her knees to her chin, staring at him intently. In the distance, there were sheep grazing.

This was no dream. This girl was the one who had saved his life. She was now bending over him and saying tenderly, "Want a fig bar?"

She held out her hand and put something soft and sweet in his mouth. Fig bar! Not bad. He nosed around for another. Meanwhile, he looked the girl over. He sniffed her. She smelled good—a combination of soap, water, freshly laundered cotton, sheep's wool, and fig bars.

"Hey. Get out of my pockets. I'll give you another one." The girl laughed, handed him another fig bar, and helped herself to one.

They sat and ate in companionable silence.

I like the way she flips her braids over her shoulder, thought Hemi.

"I thought you were done for," the girl said to him.

She has a very soft voice. It's nice on the ears, Hemi thought, as he stood up dizzily.

"What I did was to put a poultice on your mouth. It's an old Indian recipe for cactus stings. Works every time."

It is certainly better to be living, even sad as I am about Melville and all, than it is to be in those Green Pastures, Hemi thought.

"You should stay with us for a while. I mean at least until you're better."

Actually, I have no place to go now. There's no point in going back East. It's too far.

"I could take care of you."

I should stay with her if she wants me. I owe my life to her. I mean, I should try it, particularly since I seem to have lost Melville. Maybe she has some plowing to do.

"I don't see why I couldn't keep you. You could help with the herding and other things. And Mama and Papa wouldn't mind. There's always room for one more."

She is a nice person with a good smell about her, and a large supply of fig bars. Herding can't be very different from plowing. I'll stay.

So Hemi moved in with the Indian girl and her

family. When they got back to where she lived, Hemi was put into a brush corral with a little lean-to on one side of it. Here he stayed with the sheep and waited for his mouth to heal, and, as was Hemi's way, he learned a few things. He learned that the Indian girl's name was Dancing Eyes, and that her father was someone important in the tribe. He found out that the large round, earth-covered mound near his corral was called a hogan, and it was the house where Dancing Eyes lived. Hemi learned that sheep were gentle but that they smelled funny.

After his mouth healed, Hemi found out what herding was. Herding, he discovered, was when he carried Dancing Eyes on his back and they led the sheep out into the desert to graze. And then, when it was time to go home at dusk, they gathered them all up again and led them home. That was herding.

There were a lot of nice things about herding. There was standing in the shadow of a butte on a hot morning, while Dancing Eyes sat nearby, sewing. There was sharing a box of fig bars at midday. And there was walking home at sunset with the soft *baaaaing* of the sheep behind you and the orange glow of the sun in front of you. Herding, Hemi decided, was almost as nice as plowing. Besides, plowing reminded him of Melville, and he was trying to put Melville out of his mind.

A few weeks passed. Hemi began to notice something else. He noticed, for instance, that the creeks and arroyos were dry. And that he and Dancing

Eyes had to ride farther and farther into the desert to find something for the sheep to eat. And then one day there were no green patches anywhere and the daily trips into the desert stopped. Now Hemi and the sheep stayed in the little corral all day, huddled under the lean-to, trying to keep out of the blistering sun.

Hemi watched the little lizards scurrying across the roof, looking for a shady hole to hide in.

Everyone talked about rain. The Indians came to see Dancing Eyes' father and they sat and smoked and shook their heads sadly. One night, many Indians came to the hogan and they played music and danced and even the music had something to do with rain. But still there was no rain.

Dancing Eyes began to feed Hemi and the sheep from bags of food stored in a smaller hogan behind her house. She opened a bag every night and divided it among them. And she would sigh as she emptied the bag and shook it out. Hemi thought he had never seen anyone look so sad.

One day Hemi saw that there were only a few bags left in the little storeroom. That night Dancing Eyes gave them only half a bag of food to share. And Hemi noticed that while she poured it into the feeding trough something glistened on her hand.

Why, she's crying, thought Hemi. She's crying because she can't give us enough food.

That night, as Hemi lay awake listening to his growling stomach, he faced the truth:

"They haven't got enough food and I'm an extra mouth to feed. I'm not doing any herding because there's no place to herd, so what good am I? I'd be doing Dancing Eyes a favor if I left. Yes, that's what I'll do. I'll leave."

Suddenly Hemionus was wide awake. "But where will I go?" He realized that he had no place. No place to go back to and no place to go forward to.

"It used to be that I was looking for Melville, so I had a direction—wherever I thought Melville was. But now—"

At that moment, a name popped into Hemi's head. *Grand Canyon.* Grand Canyon. . . . Where had he heard that name before? . . . He searched his mule brain for a hint . . . something . . . somewhere. . . . It began to come back to him.

"I remember. . . . The notice on the board at the Agricultural College. What was it that it said? Summer students interested in the Grand Canyon project. . . . Grand Canyon! Summer students! Why hadn't he thought of that before? . . . MELVILLE. Melville might be interested in a summer project. Melville might be at the Grand Canyon. Melville. Hemi threw himself on the ground and rolled around in the dust for sheer joy, until the sheep shook their heads at such goings on. Hope was flooding back, like the rain that would soon flood the desert.

Hemi wished there was some way to tell Dancing Eyes his decision. He tried. When she came in to say good night, he rubbed his head against her and nuzzled her ear. And then he pulled at her braids in the way that made her laugh. When he did that she looked at him strangely.

"You are a dear mule," she said, hugging him. And then she sighed and went back into the house.

"Good-bye," Hemi called after her silently. "Good-bye, little Dancing Eyes. May your life be full of rain and fig bars."

He let himself out of the corral quietly, and was soon walking briskly along under a star-filled sky. "Grand Canyon," he said, "here I come."

13 *In a Fog*

"It's nice to be on my way again," Hemi said to himself cheerfully, on the first morning, as he trotted steadily in a northerly direction.

"I'm glad for Dancing Eyes' sake that it has begun to rain," he said on the second day.

"It certainly will be good for the Indians that it's raining so much," Hemi said, as his trot went into its third day.

"The truth is," said a thoroughly wet Hemi at the end of the fourth day, "I'm sick of being wet. I'm sick of traveling. I want to settle down. End my Search, under S."

"Melville," he brayed plaintively, "you'd better be

at the Grand Canyon. I don't think I can stand it if you're not."

Not only was it still raining, but now a dense fog was rolling in. Soon Hemi could hardly see two steps in front of him.

It was an eerie feeling.

He thought, Everything looks gray. Even I look gray. The fog is gray. How funny it would be if I were to dissolve, and float up the mountain as a patch of fog. Maybe it wouldn't be so bad, to be a patch of fog, moving this way and that, not thinking, not worrying about finding Melville or making the most of yourself. Going all over the world, and to Parts Unknown.

On the other hand, Hemi thought, a patch of fog could get blown away altogether, and never be heard from again. No, thank you, he decided. Being a mule is better than being fog. But not much better, he thought gloomily.

Onward and upward. Thicker and thicker fog. Now he couldn't even see the trail he was walking on, or tell whether he was going north or whether he had circled around in the fog and was heading back in the opposite direction.

He puffed, so he was sure he was going uphill.

"How is a mule supposed to know where he's going if he can't even see his hooves in front of his eyes, that's what I would like to know!

"It's all very well for Jackson to talk about the

stamina of mules while he's sitting in a nice warm stall. But it's something else again when you're trying to have stamina and stubbornness and bravery in real life. Mules do get tired and they do get discouraged," he said with a sob in his voice. "Sometimes they even feel like giving up.

"But then again," he said to himself, "is that what I'd want Jackson to tell some new young mule at the Academy?"

Hemi suddenly straightened up. "No, of course not. I would want him to say that mules never give up. That we fight on. That we win out. That we are stubborn. Stub-b-or-n."

He yelled the word into the grayness, to bolster his courage. He liked the way the sound of it drifted through the fog. So he yelled again. "Stubborn. Stubb-boooorrnn."

A sound came back to him through the fog. "Stubborn!" it cried shrilly. Was it an echo? He heard it again. "Stubborn!" Hemi was exhilarated. He was sure he had released a sound that was going to bounce around the Grand Canyon forever!

He pictured tourists standing at the rim of the canyon to see the view, suddenly hearing the splendid ringing motto of the mule floating out of the Canyon at them.

A moment later, he heard a voice above his head.

"*Who's* stubborn, is what I want to know!"

Startled, Hemionus planted his feet in preparation for a kick, should he be attacked.

"I am. Where are you and what are you?"

"I'm here in this tree and I'm a Steller's jay. Wait, I'll come down."

A large blue-and-black bird materialized out of the fog in front of Hemi.

"Hello," the jay said. "I suppose you're the one who's been yelling his head off and scaring the life out of us."

"Well, yes," said Hemi, a little embarrassed. "I'm sorry if I scared you. I was just giving myself a little pep talk. I mean, when a mule has been . . . on the road a long time . . . and looking for a friend and not finding him . . . when you're in that situation, sometimes, just sometimes, if you holler something . . . almost anything will do . . . it makes you feel a whole lot better. For a while. Sometimes . . ."

"Don't say another word. I know just what you mean. I'm all for hollering. I do it myself, all the time. Holler. Yell. Sometimes a bunch of us do it together. You can really drive a squirrel crazy that way. It makes you feel great. Where are you headed?"

"I'm trying to get to Grand Canyon. I'm looking for my friend Melville, who may be interested in a summer project around here somewhere. He's a student at the Agricultural College."

"Oh. He's probably one of those young people who have been taking tourists down the Canyon on pack trips. I flew along with some of them. It was quite interesting."

"Do you really think he may be one of the people you saw? If I describe him to you, maybe you can tell me if you've seen him."

"I doubt it. They all look alike. People, I mean. You'll have to go up to the Canyon and look for yourself."

"That's what I want to do. But I can't see where I'm going. I'll never get there at this rate."

"Oh, that. If that's your problem, I can help. I'll lead you there. Beam you in, so to speak."

"I'd be ever so much obliged," said Hemi.

"Okay, then. Here we go." The Steller's jay flew ahead, seemingly unperturbed by the fog. As he flew, he called loudly, and Hemi followed the sound of his voice.

They traveled for about an hour. And at last the jay flew back to where Hemi stood waiting to be guided farther.

"Well, here we are," he said.

"Here we are where?"

"Here we are at the rim of the Canyon."

Hemi couldn't see a thing.

"Cheer up," the jay said. "As soon as the fog lifts, you'll see the Canyon and the lodge. Then I'd advise you to look for the mule corral and get in there and look as if you belong. That way, sooner or later, you'll get to go out on a pack trip. And maybe you'll meet your friend."

"But how do you know the fog will lift?" Hemi asked.

"Always does. Either the wind will blow it away or the sun will raise the temperature and burn it off. It's called convection currents."

Hemi was impressed. "Convection currents," he repeated. "That has a nice sound. I never met a bird who knew about things like convection currents."

The jay looked down modestly and pretended to be preening his feathers. "It's nothing, really," he said. "I fly, so I have to know something about weather. And speaking of flying, I'd better be buzzing off. I'm pretty far from home and I'd like to get back before they start worrying about me."

"I wish you could stay. Just until the fog lifts."

"Not possible," said the jay. "Good luck. Be seeing you."

The Steller's jay disappeared into the fog, leaving Hemi standing at the edge of a vast white space.

"Maybe only human creatures can see the Grand Canyon," Hemi said to himself. "Or maybe you need a special pair of glasses. Maybe they have only two performances a day, like in the movies that Melville told me about. I wonder when the next show goes on."

He waited. Still no Grand Canyon. He was staring at a natural wonder of the world that was totally invisible.

After several minutes, he asked himself sadly, "How can I hope to find Melville if I can't even find the Grand Canyon?"

At that moment, a faint streak of sun began to

penetrate the fog. First Hemi felt its warmth on his back. Then, as he watched, he began to see the shape of a railing. A hotel. The Canyon Lodge.

Slowly, right before his eyes, something was emerging out of the fog. First a few peaks. Then . . . a whole landscape, stretching as far as the eye could see . . . a magic country. Rock mountains of red and green and purple and tan. A city in the clouds. Moon landscape. The deep clefts of the gorges cut through the mountains everywhere, making wide rifts and narrow chasms. And far below, like a tiny ribbon, the Colorado River wound its way along the Canyon floor.

For a long time, Hemi stood and looked. Then, at last, he said, "It's the most wonderful wonder I have ever seen. Papa was right. When I used to ask him all those questions like 'Why is life?' he said I'd have to find out why for myself. And now I've found one of them. To see the Grand Canyon is one of the reasons why life is. If only Melville were here to share it with me."

When he had finished drinking in the scenery, Hemi headed for the lodge. In no time at all, he had located the mule pen in the back. Quietly, he lifted the latch on the little corral gate, walked inside, and closed it behind him.

14 *End of the Trail*

"Well, if that don't beat all."

"If what don't beat all?"

"What's that brown mule doin' in the corral? He's not one of ours."

It was five o'clock in the afternoon. The two trail guides had just come back from their daily trip down to the bottom of the Canyon with the tourists.

They counted the mules, just to make sure.

"Nope. It don't figure. He's an extra, no matter how you look at it."

"Wonder where he came from."

"From one of the other lodges, probably. They'll be callin' us in a little while, askin' have we seen him."

The two men led the other mules into the corral,

put away the packs and saddles, filled the feed and water troughs. Then they ambled over to where Hemi was standing, to get a closer look.

"Big feller, isn't he? Must be at least sixteen hands high. I haven't seen any that big around here."

"It's hard to figure how that mule got in here."

"You know," said the taller man, "there's a pack of wild burros and horses up in the mountains. Maybe this critter is from that pack."

"But why would a wild mule come in here?"

"That's what I can't figure out. Unless . . ." the guide grinned, "he decided he wanted to be with some of his own kind."

"If that's the case he's liable to be in for a surprise. This mule pack don't take too kindly to a new one."

"Well, anyway," the shorter man said, "what are we gonna do with him?"

"Can't do anything anymore tonight. We'll leave him here until tomorrow. Then if no one calls for him we'll let one of them college boys take him over to the other lodge."

The guides walked toward their bunkhouse.

Hemi had been listening intently to their conversation. "That doesn't give me much time to find Melville. I'd better get busy."

He trotted over to where the other mules were standing.

"Hello. I'm Hemi," he said in a friendly tone. "I'm here looking for a friend. Do you mind if I join you in something to eat?"

The nearest mule lifted her lip in a snarl. "Yes," she said shortly, "we do mind."

"Who are you, anyway? You don't belong here," another mule said, in the same unfriendly tone.

Hemi hastened to explain.

"I'm just passing through. I'm looking for my friend Melville. He may be around here somewhere."

"There's no Melville in this corral," a big gray mule said curtly.

"Oh, I didn't mean right here. I meant around here. You see, Melville is . . ."

The big gray mule, who seemed to be the leader, interrupted.

"There is no mule named Melville anywhere in the Grand Canyon."

"But Melville isn't a mule," said Hemi.

"Well, then if he isn't a mule, he certainly isn't here. There are only mules on the trail . . . no horses, no donkeys . . ."

"If you'd just let me tell you . . ." Hemi was geting annoyed at the mule's attitude, and at the fact that he was standing so that Hemi couldn't get to the feed trough.

"Why don't you leave?" the big mule snarled. "You're not one of us. You don't belong here. You're not even the right color."

The other mules snorted their agreement. They began to move menacingly toward Hemi, with the big mule, whose name was Satan, in the lead.

"I really don't like this sort of thing," said Hemi

quietly. "But you should know that I am a mule who will not be put . . . UPON," he shouted, getting up on his hind legs and plunging into the group of mules.

The commotion brought the trail guides running.

"Now will you look at that," the tall man said. "Just what I was afraid of. That maverick mule has upset the whole bunch. And look what he's done to Satan!"

The lead mule, bruised and battered, had retired to a neutral corner, where he stood panting and tossing his head angrily.

Hemi stood quietly in another corner of the corral, licking a small cut on his nose and thinking about how you couldn't necessarily depend on fellow-mules to be friendly.

"All right," he heard the trail guide say. "That settles it. We'll have to get the big brown out of here tonight. He's a troublemaker."

"Now *that's* unfair," Hemi brayed angrily. "Blaming it on me. They weren't even here to see what happened. Well, I'm not going. I'm staying right here until tomorrow, and see if I can find Melville."

When the trail guide came up to him, Hemi looked fierce and pawed the ground.

The guide circled him cautiously. Then he hitched up his jeans and moved in to grab him.

As Hemi watched the guide pick himself up from the ground, he sighed. "I hope he isn't hurt. He really isn't a bad man . . . it's just that I'm not ready to leave this place yet. I have a feeling that . . ."

He stopped to watch the two guides swinging a lasso in his direction. Hemi ducked agilely whenever the rope came near.

"I didn't come all the way across country without learning a little bit about a lasso," he said, as the two men tried time and again to rope him.

Hemi eluded the men for two hours. Finally, the taller of the two men threw down his hat in disgust.

"Stubborn cuss. He just don't want to be caught!"

"Tell you what," the other guide said. "Why don't we get that college kid . . . you know, the one with the bushy hair who's so good with animals. Mebbe he can do something with this durned mule."

It was nearly dark when Hemi heard them coming back.

The first glimpse he got of him was a slim figure vaulting over the corral fence.

Hemi peered into the darkness. It was hard to see but . . . there was something about that outline . . . that way of moving . . . those patched jeans . . . that shape . . . that faint smell of chocolate candy. . . . Could it be? Could it possibly be? MELVILLE! IT WAS MELVILLE!

"Hullo," said Melville softly. "What's this we got here? Big brown mule. Where'd you come from, man? You look like the mules from my hometown."

He doesn't know me, thought Hemi.

Melville came closer. Hemi trembled with excitement.

"Come on over to the light and let's have a look at you."

Hemi trotted joyfully behind Melville. The trail guides looked on, astonished.

"Now. Let's see you, big guy. My, you got a peck of dirt on you, man. You look like you been on a long trip."

Now Melville held Hemi's head and looked into his face.

"Man, you sure look like a mule I used to know. I wonder what happened to that mule," he whispered softly. And then Melville glanced down. In the darkness he saw it . . . the white star-shaped mark on Hemi's fetlock joint.

At that moment, Hemi reached into Melville's shirt pocket, pulled out the Oh Henry bar that only he could know was there, and ate it, paper and all.

That did it.

"Hemi?" Melville said softly. "Hemi. Is it really you? Yes. It is. HEMI!"

What a reunion it was! After the hugging and the nuzzling and the talking and the knee-biting and the candy-eating were about over, Melville explained the whole thing to the guides, and introduced them to Hemi, who was just as polite as he had been unfriendly before. Then they all went up to the bunkhouse and Melville got his sleeping bag and he and Hemi went up into the woods and bedded down under the stars together.

Soon the moon came up. Hemi stood in the grove of trees, sniffing the wonderful smells of evergreens and Melville. He looked down at the dear familiar shape of his friend. Melville was talking to him softly. . . .

"Man, we are going to do so many things together. First, this summer, I'll teach you how to be a trail mule. Wait till you go down that Canyon trail. Why, if you keep your eyes open you can see so many things—mountain lions, mule deer, antelope, gray fox, gophers, horned toads . . . it's one of the wonders of the world, that Canyon.

"And, Hemionus, when I go back to college, I'm gonna take you with me. There's plenty of room for a mule on the Experimental Range. You're gonna be a college mule, man. One thing for sure. It's just gonna be you and me, from now on. Makin' the most of it."

Hemi sighed contentedly. It was turning out just like Mama said.